First-Start® Legends

WHY OWL COMES OUT AT NIGHT

A STORY FROM HAITI

Retold by Janet Palazzo-Craig   Illustrated by Charles Reasoner

Troll

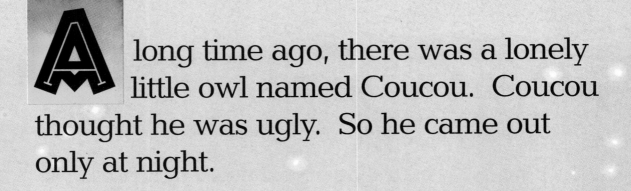A long time ago, there was a lonely little owl named Coucou. Coucou thought he was ugly. So he came out only at night.

4

One afternoon, Coucou was sleeping. Suddenly, a hummingbird flew straight into him. The hummingbird cried, "How ugly you are!" Then off she flew.

"Oh, no," said Coucou. "Just as I thought—I *am* ugly."

Coucou looked into a pond to see himself. *Zip!* Away swam a little fish. "I am so ugly, I scare even the fish," he said.

So Coucou hid himself away.
He came out only when there
was no moonlight.

One night, Coucou heard
someone crying. In a nearby
bush, he saw a beautiful
swallow.

"What is wrong?" asked Coucou.

"I am lost," said the swallow. "I can't find my way home in the dark."

Coucou could see very well in the dark. So he took the swallow, whose name was Drina, back to her home.

Drina liked the friendly owl. Soon she was no longer sad.

Coucou was glad it was dark. Drina could not see his face.

The next night, Drina came to find Coucou. How surprised he was!

They talked and laughed for hours. They were soon good friends.

One night, Drina told Coucou, "I will give a party for you." Coucou was delighted!

But later he realized there would be a full moon on the night of the party. *"Coo-whoo!"* he cried. "Drina will see how ugly I am!"

Coucou asked Rouge the rooster for advice. "Wear my big hat," said Rouge. "It will cover your face.

"I will come to the party with you. I will tell you when dawn is coming." But to himself, Rouge thought, "And while you are hiding, I will meet the beautiful Drina."

The night of the party came. "Coucou!" said Drina. "Come and dance!"

Coucou loved dancing with Drina so much that he forgot about his ugliness.

After a while, Coucou became tired. "I must rest," he told Drina. "Rouge will dance with you."

That was just what the rooster wanted to hear! "Yes," said Rouge. "Don't worry, Coucou. I will tell you when dawn is coming."

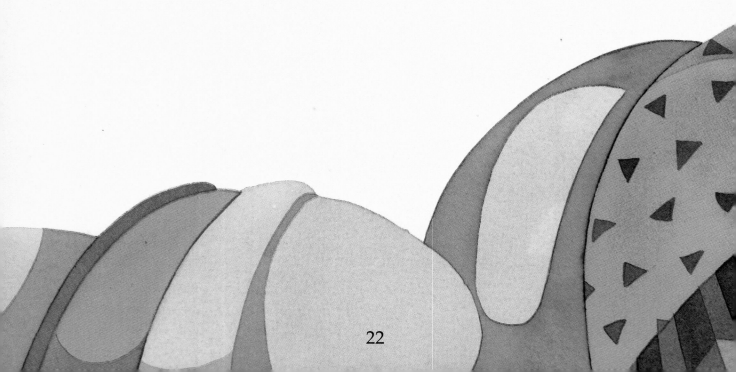

Soon the owl was fast asleep.

As Coucou slept, Rouge tried to charm Drina. But she paid him no mind.

The rooster decided to trick Coucou. He would let the dawn come without telling the owl. Then Coucou would run and hide. Rouge would have Drina all to himself!

The rooster did just that.
"Cock-a-doodle-doo!" he crowed at dawn.

Coucou awoke suddenly. His hat
fell off. Everyone saw him!

27

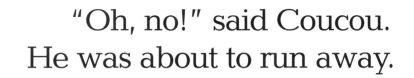

"Oh, no!" said Coucou.
He was about to run away.

But then he thought of
something. How could Drina
ever love him unless she
knew all about him—even
about his ugly face?

He turned his face to
Drina. Her eyes were full
of love! "Why have you
hidden under that hat all
night?" she said. And the
two began to dance.

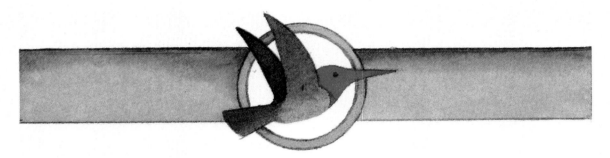

From that time on, Coucou never hid
his face from his lovely Drina, no
matter how bright the light of the moon!

The Caribbean Islands

Florida

Haiti

Why Owl Comes Out at Night is a folktale from the Caribbean country of Haiti. On Christmas Day, 1492, Christopher Columbus was shipwrecked on Haiti. He used the ship's timber to build a fort, which he called Fort Navidad. Today, Haiti is populated by the descendants of former slaves. They speak a form of French known as Haitian Creole.

WHY OWL COMES OUT AT NIGHT

DEC 1997

W1